Practice Makes Perfect

MPress books

PRACTICE MAKES PERFECT

First published in 2017 by M*Press* Books

MPress Books Limited Reg. No 6379441 is a company registered in Great Britain
Tall Grass Productions is an imprint of MPress Books Limited
www.mpressbooks.co.uk

British Library Cataloguing in Publication Data
A catalogue record for this book is available from the British Library.

ISBN

978-0-9930384-8-8

Typeset in Two Fingers Bodoni
Origination by Core Creative, Yeovil 01935 477453

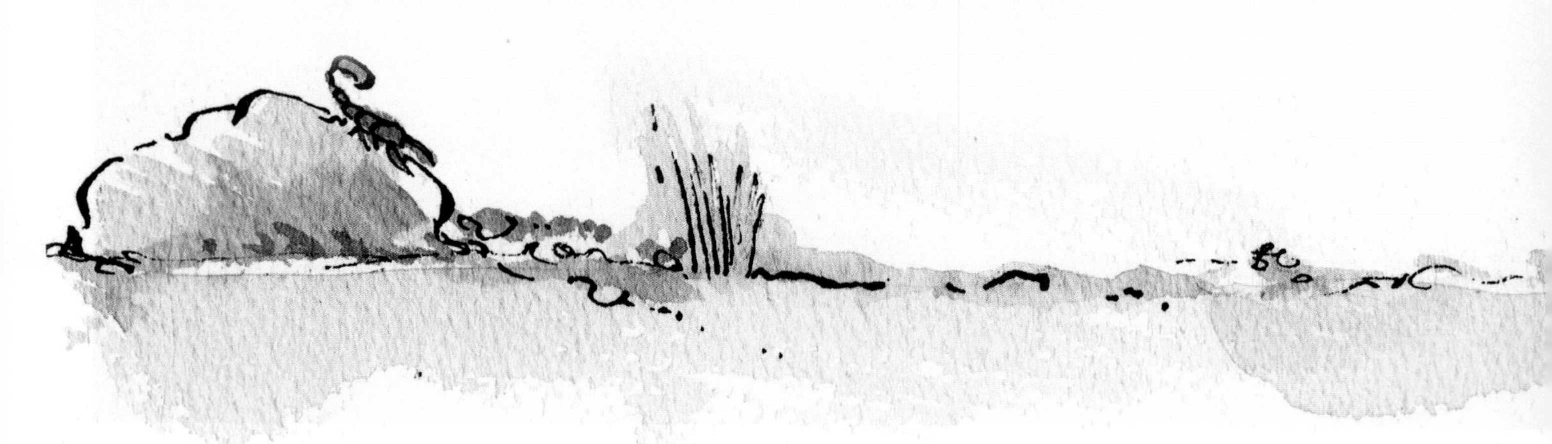

Practice Makes Perfect

This book belongs to...

Illustrated by Maria Floyd
Written by Clare Luther

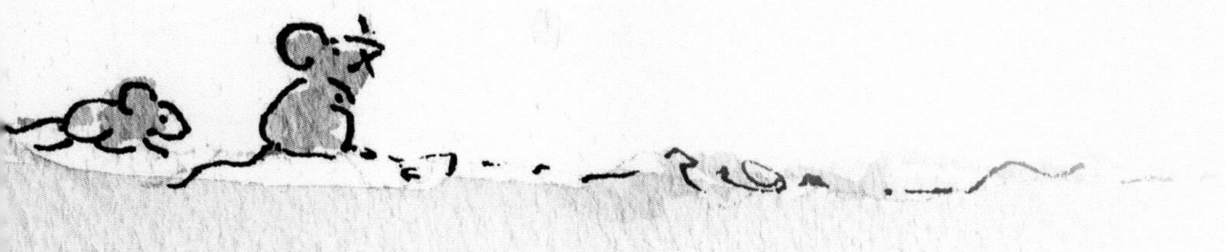

The slow porcupine who waddled and whined, was a rodent much **bigger** than most.

Neither quick nor slight
and certainly not light,
his home was the
red desert coast.

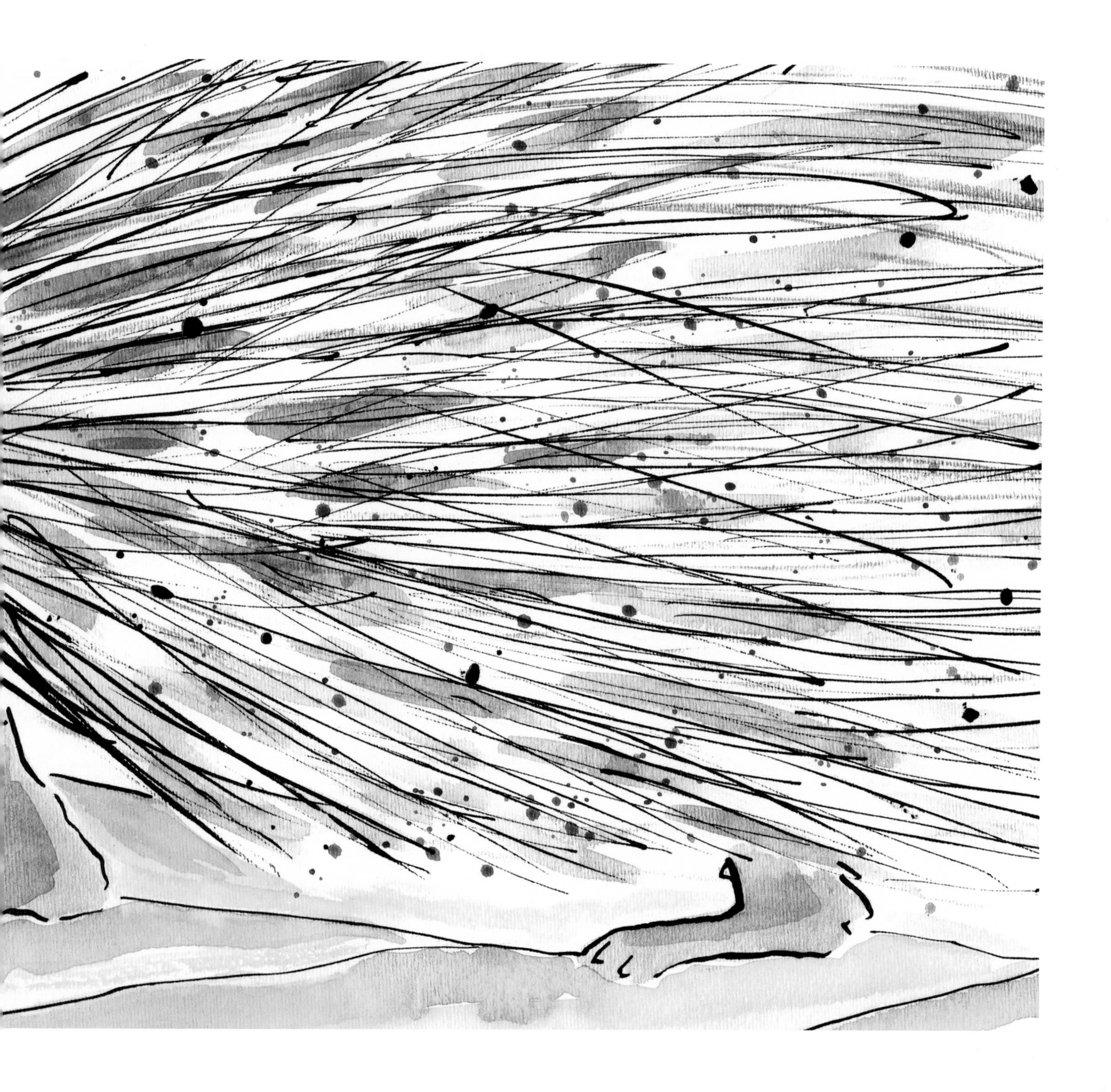

From dawn to dark he would sleep in the bark
of an empty and OLD TREE ROOT.

His black and white spikes were tucked up all tight,
he LOVED to snooze - HOW CUTE!

He would grunt and SNORT without worry or THOUGHT, sleeping soundly throughout the whole DAY.

Secure in his DEN, he would stir now and THEN, only rising at night time to PLAY.

With his needle like fur all his friends would prefer
to keep a good distance from HIM.

It was never their will to get stuck on a quill
as they knew it was PAINFUL and GRIM.

Yet strangely enough when he tried to look TOUGH and FRIGHTEN attackers away,

his spikes would stay *flat*, keeping close to his back;
they refused to **spring** up and stay.

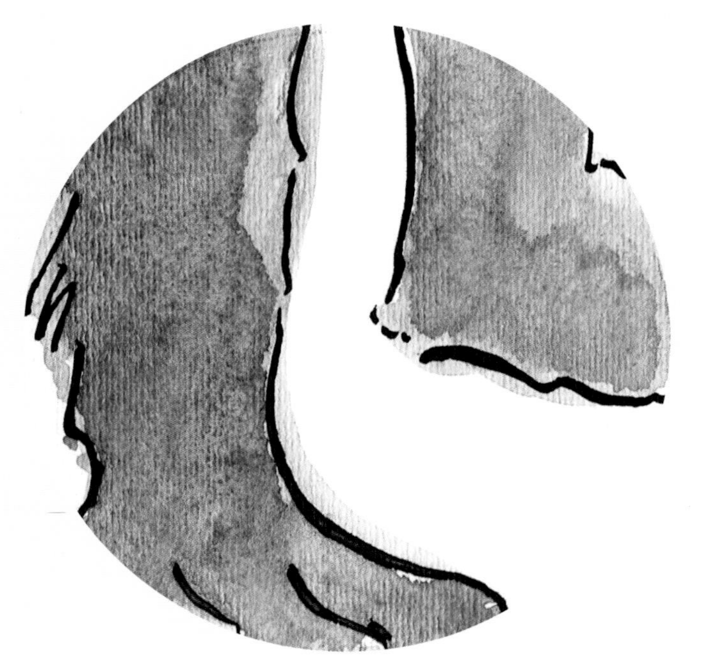

He could STAMP his feet, THRASH his tail with a beat,

and run backwards to cause a GREAT SCARE.

Yet his coat did
not MOVE; when he
froze it stayed SMOOTH,

not a SPIKE
went up in
the AIR.

Sleeping all afternoon on the RED ROLLING DUNES
he would wake to practise at NIGHT.

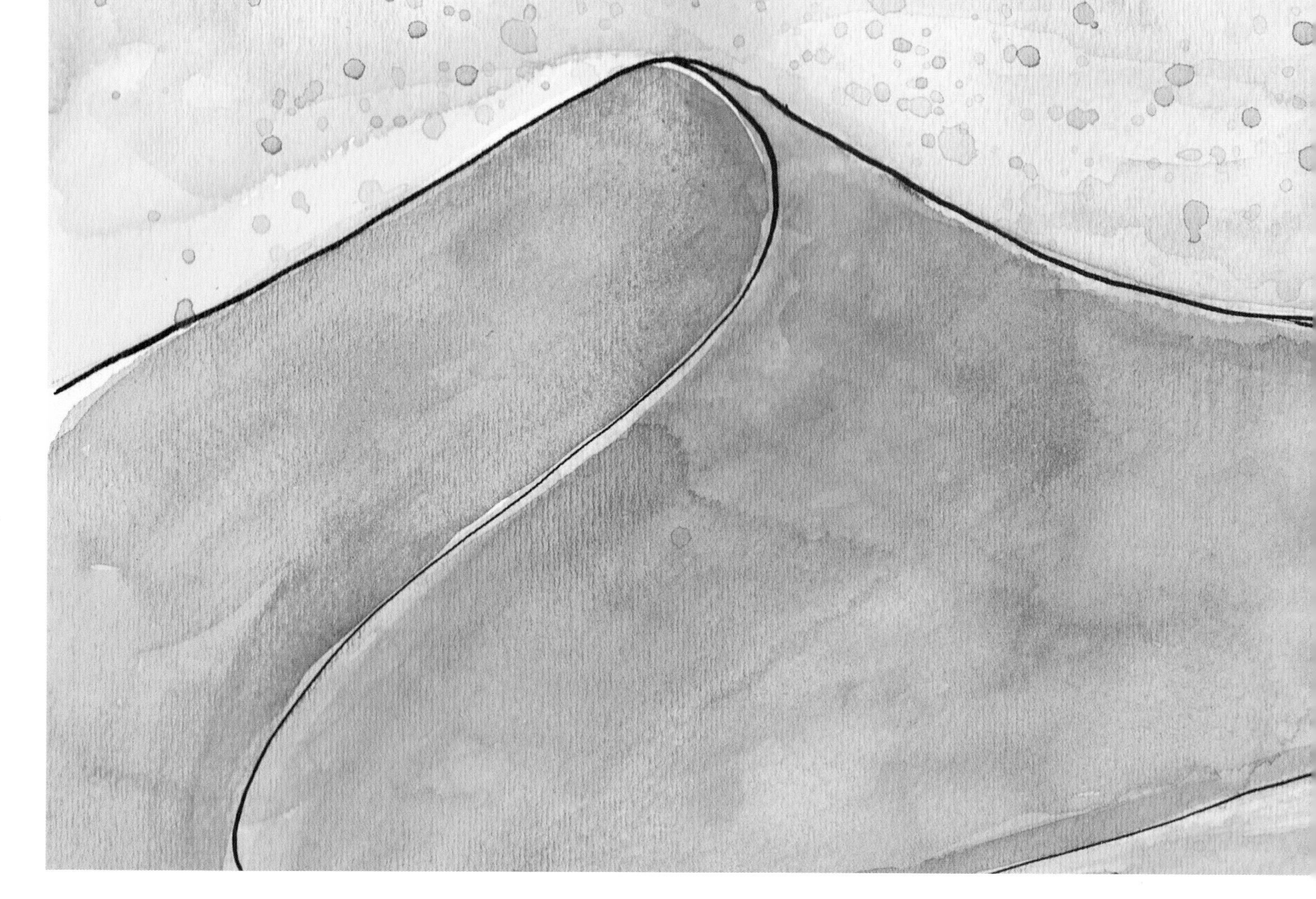

So determined was he to make enemies FLEE,

that he worked with EFFORT and MIGHT.

When dark he would BATTLE to make his spikes RATTLE -
there was nothing, they just stuck to the FLOOR.
He trained ever so HARD to keep up his GUARD -
with no luck he would then try some MORE.

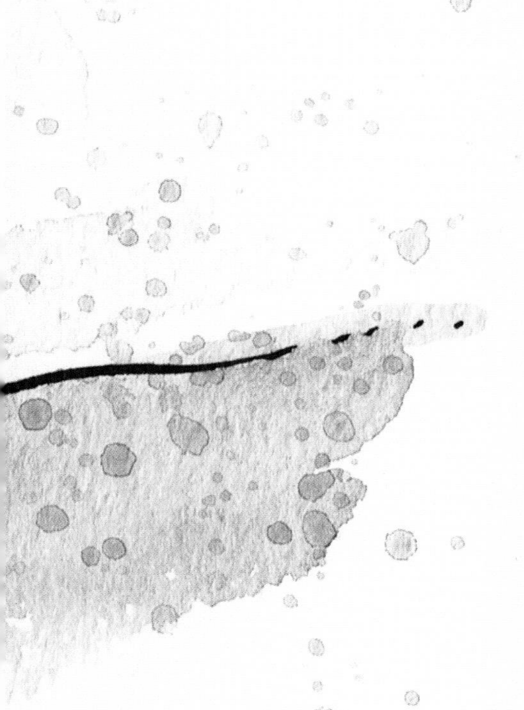

From a web-footed gecko
came a FAINT LITTLE ECHO that blew
with the wind from BEHIND.

He chirped from the DUNE,
which shone in the MOON,
"You can do it, just focus
your MIND!"

"Learn how to protect your body from threat,
just pretend you are under ATTACK.
Have a go once again... KEEP GOING my friend,
try **lifting** those SPIKES off your BACK."

With that picture in mind the young porcupine continued to push on some MORE.

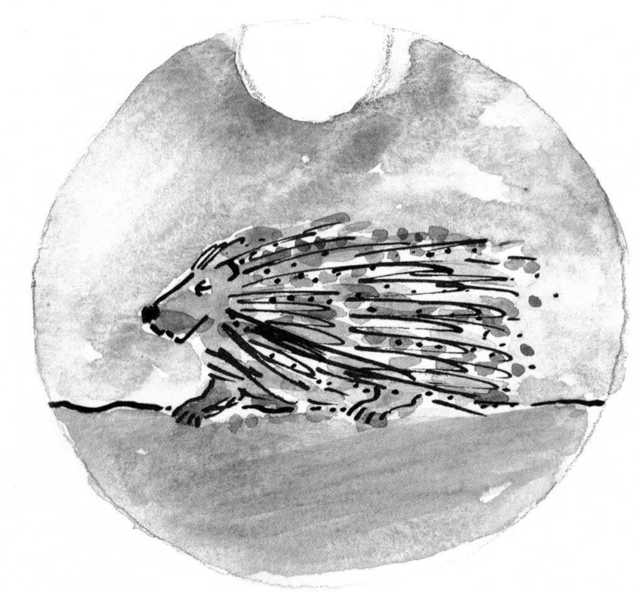

He tried again... and again... and again... AND again - he kept going until he was SORE!

Then one eerie night he
had a true FRIGHT -
a cheetah was prowling nearby.

In the blink of an EYE his quills went SKY HIGH,

the cheetah ran off -

goodbyeeeee!

"WOW, practice makes perfect
and my effort was worth it!"
the porcupine gleefully smiled.

"I am glad I kept going, it's so
WONDERFUL knowing that I'm
SAFE out here in the WILD."

Clare Luther

She studied Occupational Therapy at Oxford Brookes University. She worked as an Occupational Therapist and Life Coach, in both the public and private sector, until 2013. Clare now has a diverse work life where she continues to use her skills in a variety of settings. She has held a passion for writing poetry since her teenage years. She lives in London with her husband and two children.

Maria Floyd

She studied Fine Art and History of Art at Goldsmiths' College, London and is a successful painter and illustrator. She has held several exhibitions of her work in the UK and divides her time between Somerset and North Cornwall. She lives with her husband and three children.